Riding
School Rivals

RIDING SCHOOL RIVALS

*The story of a majestic Lipizzan horse
and the girls who fight for the right to ride him*

Written by **Susan Saunders**
Illustrated by **Sandy Rabinowitz**
Cover Illustration by **Christa Keiffer**
Developed by Nancy Hall, Inc.

Gareth Stevens Publishing
MILWAUKEE

For a free color catalog describing Gareth Stevens' list of high-quality books and
multimedia programs, call 1-800-542-2595 (USA) or 1-800-461-9120 (Canada).
Gareth Stevens Publishing's Fax: (414) 225-0377.

Library of Congress Cataloging-in-Publication Data

Saunders, Susan.
Riding school rivals / written by Susan Saunders; illustrated by
Sandy Rabinowitz; cover illustration by Christa Keiffer.
p. cm.
Originally published: Dyersville, Iowa: Ertl Co., 1996.
(Treasured horses collection)
Summary: Cassie and Hillary vie with each other
for the privilege of riding Birchwood Stable's new
Lipizzan horse in an important horse show.
ISBN 0-8368-2281-1 (lib. bdg.)
[1. Interpersonal relations—Fiction. 2. Lipizzaner horse—
Fiction. 3. Horses—Fiction.] I. Rabinowitz, Sandy, ill. II. Title.
III. Series: Treasured horses collection.
PZ7.S2577Rg 1999
[Fic]—dc21   98-46305

This edition first published in 1999 by
Gareth Stevens Publishing
1555 North RiverCenter Drive, Suite 201
Milwaukee, Wisconsin 53212 USA

© 1996 by Nancy Hall, Inc. First published by Scholastic Inc., New York,
New York, by arrangement with Nancy Hall, Inc. and The ERTL Company.

Printed in the United States of America

1 2 3 4 5 6 7 8 9 03 02 01 00 99

CONTENTS

The Girls at Birchwood Stable

Cassie Sinclair had taken hundreds of riding lessons over the past four and a half years. But she knew that she could take thousands more and never get tired of them.

Cassie was eleven. She figured she would still be riding when she was forty years old. Or fifty. Or maybe even sixty! And there would always be something new for her to learn.

Every Saturday morning at ten o' clock, Cassie, her best friend Amy Lin, Sara Gerson, and a new girl named Hillary Craig took group lessons from Trisha Prescott at Birchwood Stable.

Riding was Cassie's passion. Besides the group

lesson every Saturday, she had a private lesson in jumping on Sundays. And when she wasn't riding, she was thinking about riding.

Cassie daydreamed about jumping in the Olympics someday. But if she ended up half as good a rider as Trisha Prescott, Cassie would be happy.

Trisha owned Birchwood. She knew more about horses, and riding, than anyone Cassie had ever met. Trisha had been a champion hunter rider and had trained dozens of horses that had become winners. Not only was Trisha a terrific rider and horse trainer, she was a wonderful teacher as well. She didn't put up with any nonsense from students or horses. But Trisha was patient, and she was always fair.

Right now, Trisha was standing at one end of the indoor ring at Birchwood. She was always perfectly turned out, even when she was just hanging around the barn. Today, Trisha was wearing spotless beige jodhpurs, brown paddock boots, a blue-and-white pin-striped shirt, and a dark-brown leather belt with a sterling silver buckle.

Trisha had wavy brownish-blond hair and clear gray eyes that never missed a thing. Right now they were trained on Amy and Freckles as Amy put her horse through his paces. Amy had been taking lessons for two years. It had been hard for her at first, because she was a little afraid of horses. But the horse she rode, Freckles, was one of the smaller horses at Birchwood. He was small and round. That was fine with Amy, who was short and round herself.

Waiting their turn near the gate were Cassie, Sara, and Hillary on their horses. Cassie was watching Amy intently as she trotted around the ring. Even when she wasn't riding, just watching the other girls in her Saturday group and listening to Trisha taught Cassie a lot.

Cassie was blessed with a straight back and long legs that made her look great on a horse. She had skin the color of coffee ice cream and long, black hair that she wore in a thick braid. Gold earrings in the shape of tiny horseshoes gleamed in her ears.

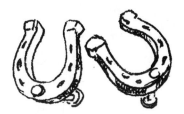

At Birchwood Stable, Cassie had been riding a chestnut mare named Allegra for the past two years. Allegra was a dependable horse, and she tried hard. But now that Cassie was getting more advanced in jumping, she wished that Allegra were younger and livelier.

On one side of Cassie and Allegra, Sara Gerson fiddled with her reins. Sara was ten, and a year behind the other girls in school. She was small, with a pale, heart-shaped face and shoulder-length dark hair. She rode a neat bay horse named Charlie that her parents were thinking about leasing for her.

Sara had been taking lessons from Trisha for three years. She was a much better rider than she gave herself credit for. But she had terrible stage fright. She even got nervous riding in front of her Saturday group.

Hillary Craig was eleven, the same age as Cassie and Amy. But she was a bigger girl, taller and heavier than Cassie, with reddish-brown hair that she pulled back into a ponytail.

Hillary was a good rider. She was quick to announce to the other girls that she had been riding almost since the time she could walk!

Hillary had recently moved to Maryland from California. She had been taking group lessons from Trisha for a couple of months, long enough to annoy practically everyone at the stable with her snooty attitude.

Hillary took private lessons in jumping, too. Her class was right after Cassie's private jumping lesson on Sundays. Usually, Hillary made a point of arriving early to watch Cassie and Allegra work.

At first, Cassie thought that maybe it was Hillary's way of trying to make friends. But when Cassie tried to talk to Hillary, the girl could barely be bothered to answer. So Cassie decided that Hillary came early just to keep an eye on her.

Hillary definitely felt she had an edge over Cassie and Allegra because of Bliss. Bliss was the black gelding Hillary rode at Birchwood. He was young and strong and a good jumper.

"Hillary doesn't want to be friends, Cassie," Amy Lin had said more than once. "I think she's trying to jinx you!"

"Amy, let's see your trot," Trisha was saying now. "Shorten your reins."

Amy tightened her reins a little more. She squeezed her legs once to make Freckles pay attention, then twice more to speed him up.

As soon as Freckles trotted, Amy began to post. She leaned forward slightly and let the horse's movements raise her out of the saddle on the first beat. On the second beat, she lowered herself.

"Easy now," Trisha called out to Amy. "Please don't bounce, or you'll lose your balance. Keep your heels down . . . down. And look straight ahead, Amy, not down at Freckles."

Amy giggled. She had heard all of these

instructions many, many times. As she had said to Cassie, though, "I can't be expected to remember everything, can I?"

Cassie had smiled with her friend.

Now she heard a loud, cranky sigh coming from her right. It was Hillary, letting everyone know that her valuable time was being wasted.

Not satisfied with just sighing, Hillary leaned toward Cassie to mutter, "I can't see why you hang around with that girl. What if her bad riding rubs off on you?"

"Amy is my best friend! And she is trying really hard!" Cassie whispered, her eyes still on Amy and Freckles. Trisha expected everyone in the group to pay strict attention.

But instead of watching Amy, or listening to Trisha, Hillary hummed loudly and stared down at the toe of her boot.

"Let's try a canter now," Trisha said to Amy. "Sit deep and tall."

Amy nudged Freckles again, and he broke into the "one-two-three" beat of the canter. Amy sat back in the saddle and rocked along, enjoying herself.

"You're looking good," Trisha called out. "Okay . . . take hold . . . slow him down . . . now . . . stop."

Amy brought Freckles to a halt.

"Back up," said Trisha.

Amy squeezed on the reins . . . let up . . . squeezed . . . let up. Freckles took a few steps backward.

"Well done," Trisha said to Amy. "Sara, let's have a look at you next."

Another loud sigh escaped from Hillary as Sara rode into the center of the ring.

"What's her problem?" Amy murmured to Cassie, turning Freckles around beside the gate.

"I guess she's bored," Cassie whispered back.

"So why does the great Hillary Craig take group lessons, if we're so boring?" Amy said in a louder voice.

Cassie had wondered about that herself. Why didn't Hillary just take two jumping lessons instead? She certainly didn't seem to be getting anything out of her group riding lessons.

"Quiet, girls, please!" said Trisha, without taking her eyes off Sara.

Sara immediately lost her left stirrup and had to grab the front of her saddle to keep from slipping sideways.

Sara blushed bright red. Cassie could see it even in the low light of the indoor ring.

Hillary snorted and stared at the ceiling.

13

"That's okay, Sara," Trisha said. "Why don't we try posting to the trot without stirrups? It's great for balance."

Sara nodded, pulling her right foot out of the stirrup, too. "Wait. I think everyone should do it," said Trisha. "Cassie, you go first. Then Hillary, next Amy, and Sara at the end."

The four of them crossed their stirrup leathers in front of their saddles to get them out of the way. Then the four girls formed a line, as in follow-the-leader.

"Legs under your body, knees bent, calves against your horse's sides, toes higher than heels," Trisha said. "Eyes straight ahead. And let your horse lift you into the post."

Posting without stirrups wasn't easy. But it was a great exercise for balance, muscle control, and learning to move with the horse, all of which Cassie needed for jumping.

She and Allegra were circling smoothly around the ring when suddenly the mare jumped forward. Cassie lowered her hands to Allegra's neck to steady herself. And she stopped posting.

Allegra bounced forward again. Cassie glanced briefly to one side, and there was Bliss's head, about to bump against Allegra's rump! Was Hillary trying to run over her?

"Hillary, take hold of Bliss!" Trisha called out sharply.

"Sorry. He can't stand not to be first!" Hillary called back.

"And neither can you!" Cassie felt like yelling at Hillary. But she didn't. Trisha liked things at the stable to go smoothly. More than once, Cassie had heard Trisha say, "Don't let personalities get in the way of your riding."

"Well, our hour is up anyway. Slow down . . . and stop," Trisha said to the girls now.

She walked over to open the gate for them to ride out. "Girls, Robert is away for the morning"—Robert Martin was Trisha's stablehand—"and I would really appreciate it if you could help me out by grooming your horses before you go," she added.

"Sure," Cassie and Amy said together.

Cassie's mom would be picking them up that day. But the Sinclairs' house was only a couple of miles from the stable. And Mrs. Sinclair usually waited for Cassie to call her on the phone, because Cassie often liked to spend extra time at Birchwood after her lessons were over.

"I'll help, too," said Sara.

But Hillary said, "Sorry, Trisha, I can't. I've got a dentist appointment." And she nudged Bliss through the gate ahead of the other horses.

Amy rolled her eyes at Cassie, meaning, "Oh, right! The truth is that Hillary is just too good to groom her horse with the rest of us!"

"Please unsaddle Bliss before you go, Hillary," Trisha said. Then she said to Cassie, "I wanted you to hang around for a while, anyway, Cassie. I hope to have a surprise for you later this morning."

"A surprise for me?" said Cassie, puzzled. "What kind of surprise?"

Hillary tugged on Bliss and paused to listen.

Trisha just smiled at Cassie. "I think you'll be pleased," was all she said.

CHAPTER
TWO

Majesty

The four girls led their horses into the barn, where Hillary exchanged Bliss's bridle for a halter. She hitched the lead rope to a cross tie and then walked away with only a wave to the others.

"And thanks for helping out, Hillary," Amy muttered.

Cassie, Amy, and Sara put halters on their horses, too. Then the girls unsaddled all four horses and led them out of the barn to the grooming tree. The grooming tree was a spreading oak, comfortably shady on even the warmest days.

Trisha carried out brushes and curry combs. "I'll bring a bucket of warm water for their tails," she told the girls as she walked away.

Cassie, Amy, and Sara got started on Allegra, Freckles, and Sara's horse, Charlie, with rubber curry combs and body brushes.

"I can't figure Hillary out," Cassie said as they worked. "She says she's been riding for years, so she must really love it. But if she loves it, why doesn't she seem to care about her horse, or learning anything from Trisha, or . . . "

"I don't think Hillary loves riding. I think she loves winning!" Amy declared, circling Freckles's back with a curry comb.

"Maybe Hillary just hates losing," Sara said suddenly. "My parents met her parents at a party last week."

Sara so rarely spoke that Cassie and Amy both stopped brushing to give her their full attention.

"My mom said that Mrs. Craig talked the whole time about the prizes Hillary won in shows in California," Sara told them. "And how Hillary is just like her dad."

"Her dad rides, too?" Cassie said. Sometimes she wished her dad or mom were more interested in riding.

"Um-hmm. Mrs. Craig is sure that Hillary will make enough points to go to the big horse shows at the end of the summer," Sara went on.

"Cassie's a hundred times better rider than Hillary is!" Amy said huffily.

"I don't know about a hundred times," Cassie said, smiling at her friend. "What else did Hillary's mom say, Sara?"

"That she and Mr. Craig talked to Trisha about finding Hillary a really special horse to jump on," Sara said. "They'll lease it or maybe even buy it for her."

Cassie allowed herself a small sigh.

Riding lessons were expensive enough. Buying a horse was too much for the Sinclairs' budget. And even leasing a horse would be a big expense for Cassie's parents.

In the hunter classes at horse shows, the classes in which many of Trisha's students competed, it was the horse that was judged, not the rider. And if Hillary had a great horse . . . Cassie was afraid that she and Allegra might be left in the dust. And she had to admit she wanted to beat Hillary.

"What about Mr. Craig? Did he have anything to say?" Amy was asking.

Sara shook her head. "No. Just Mrs. Craig, talking about what a great rider he was when he was younger and had the time to train for horse shows."

"And Hillary wants to follow in his footsteps,"

Cassie said. Just then, she heard a horse trailer rattling down the lane leading to the stables. The rattling grew louder and louder.

Allegra, Freckles, Charlie, and Bliss all raised their heads to listen, their ears perked.

"It sounds like Trisha's horse trailer," Sara said.

Sure enough, Robert Martin pulled Trisha's blue trailer into the parking area beside the barn. Trisha hurried outside, spoke to Robert for a second, and peeked inside the trailer. Then she waved to the three girls.

"Come take a look!" Trisha called to them.

They dropped their combs and brushes and rushed over. When they reached the trailer, Robert had opened the door and fixed the ramp.

"Is it a new horse for Birchwood?" Amy asked Trisha.

"A very special horse," Trisha said, adding, "and I think that Cassie will be one of the few students riding him."

"Me?" Cassie practically shrieked.

"You've gone as far as you can with Allegra," said Trisha. "It's time for you to trade up, and this might be the right horse for you."

"Excellent, Cassie!" said Amy.

Now Cassie was so excited she could hardly

breathe! She tried to imagine what the new horse would look like.

There was a clatter of hooves inside the trailer.

"Here he comes," said Trisha.

Robert walked out of the trailer, holding the lead rope. Just behind him was the most beautiful horse Cassie had ever seen. He was beyond anything she could have imagined!

The horse was a gleaming, milky white. His legs were short and strong, his body powerful. He had a heavy, arched neck, a large head, and huge brown eyes that shone with intelligence. The horse stepped proudly out of the trailer as if he were a king and Birchwood was his new kingdom.

"He's gorgeous!" Amy gasped.

Cassie could only nod in agreement. She still hadn't found her tongue.

"Girls, meet Majesty. He's a Lipizzan," Trisha said.

"Wow, a Lipizzan! I thought all the Lipizzans were in Austria, at the Spanish Riding School," said Sara, who had read practically every book ever written about horses.

"There are a few Lipizzans in the United States," said Trisha. "They're wonderful dressage horses, and they're excellent jumpers, too."

"Jumpers?" a voice said from behind them.

It was Hillary, still hanging around. Her curiosity had gotten the best of her.

"Is this my new horse?" she asked Trisha quickly. "The one my parents asked you to find for me to jump on?"

Cassie's heart sank. What if this wonderful horse wasn't going to be hers to ride, after all?

"I thought you had a dentist appointment, Hillary," Trisha said dryly. She added, "No, this isn't your horse. Majesty will be a Birchwood horse. And Cassie will be riding him if they're a good match."

"Oh, we will be." Cassie felt like shouting it. "I just know we will!"

By a "good match," Trisha was talking about personalities, as well as size and strength of horse and rider. A less experienced rider, like Amy, should have a horse that is slow and steady, like Freckles. A nervous rider should have an even-tempered horse, like Sara and Charlie. Trisha was good at matching horses and riders so that it worked out best for both.

But Hillary's face had settled into a scowl. "And what if they're *not* a good match?"

She was working herself up into a real snit.

"It's not fair! I'm a better rider than anyone here!" Hillary said, glaring at Cassie. "I've got more ribbons already than any of these girls will ever have! You're

24

just playing favorites. I deserve the best horse!"

"I'm looking for the right horse for you, Hillary. And in the meantime, you're already riding Bliss," Trisha pointed out. "Bliss is a very good jumper."

"Let Cassie ride Bliss, then, if he's so good!" Hillary yelled.

Trisha frowned. "Hillary, I have heard enough," she said quietly but sternly. "I will not permit a student to tell me how to run Birchwood Stable."

"But . . . ," Hillary began. She was glancing around as if she were looking for someone. "Mom? Mom!"

A car door slammed at the far end of the barn, and a tall blond woman walked quickly toward them.

"Mom, speak to Trisha for me," Hillary ordered, when her mother was within earshot. "I want this horse!"

"He looks nice," Mrs. Craig said, glancing at Majesty. "Of course, your father will also want to see him before we decide."

"Mrs. Craig," Trisha said, "I bought this horse to use here at the stable. I am looking for a jumper for your daughter, and I'm . . ."

"Mom!" Hillary whined. "I want Majesty!"

"Can you believe this?" Amy murmured to Cassie.

And Sara was so embarrassed by all the fuss that she looked ready to sink through the ground.

Now Trisha was really annoyed. "Mrs. Craig, we'll talk about this in my office," she said firmly. Then she turned to Cassie, Amy, and Sara, and added, "Thanks for helping with the grooming, girls. Robert will finish up."

"Nuts!" Amy whispered to Cassie. "I wanted to hear the end of this!"

"So did I," Cassie said. After all, she had the most to lose. Or gain.

But she headed toward the tack room and the pay phone to call her mother.

Cassie wouldn't know until the next day if the Lipizzan was hers to ride. Or if she'd already lost Majesty to Hillary Craig.

Trouble with Hillary

Amy had lunch at Cassie's house that day. The two of them told Cassie's mom and dad all about Majesty—and about Hillary.

Mr. Sinclair said, "Hillary may still be adjusting to the move from California. It's a big change to leave your home so far behind and move to a new place where you don't know anyone."

"Well, maybe that's part of it," Cassie said. "But Hillary doesn't seem to want to know anyone. When she first arrived, we were all friendly to her. When the theater had that film festival on horses, I invited her to go with Amy and me, but she said she was busy."

"Maybe she *was* busy," Mrs. Sinclair said.

"And I invited her to my birthday party," Amy said. "She never showed up."

"Finally we got tired of inviting her. It was clear she didn't want to be friends with us," Cassie said.

"And she's horribly jealous of Cassie," Amy said. "Hillary hates it that Cassie is such a good rider."

"Hillary's a good rider, too," said Cassie, trying to be fair.

"But that's not enough for Hillary," Amy said. "She has to be the *only* good rider at Birchwood. Or maybe in the world!"

Sometimes Amy did exaggerate. And Cassie could see from her parents' expressions that they couldn't completely accept what Amy was telling them.

"At any rate, Trisha Prescott has already made her decision about the Lipizzan," Mr. Sinclair said to Cassie. "She told you that you would be riding Majesty. If I know Trisha, she's not going to go back on her word."

Cassie hoped he was right. But she supposed that Mrs. Craig could be very stubborn, if she was anything like Hillary. And Trisha hated conflict at the stable. Would she give in to the Craigs to smooth over an unpleasant situation?

Before Cassie biked to Birchwood for her jumping lesson the next day, her mother said, "Don't give up on

Hillary. Try to be nicer to her, and she might warm up to you."

"Okay, Mom. I'll try," Cassie said.

But she knew in her heart that Hillary Craig was not at all interested in having Amy and her for pals. Hillary seemed to have a one-track mind that didn't allow for friends at Birchwood.

Cassie's Sunday lessons began at two o'clock. She was usually so eager to start that she got to the stable fifteen or twenty minutes early. This Sunday, Cassie biked over a half hour early.

Amy was waiting for her under the grooming tree.

"What are you doing here?" Cassie asked, delighted to see her friend.

"I thought you might need me here for some support," Amy said. "And I'm glad I came. We're not alone."

"Who's here?" Cassie glanced around the paddock, where some of the horses were running and playing in the sunshine. Then she looked at the two outdoor rings. She would be having her jumping lesson in the nearer one. The jumps were already set up. "Check the gazebo," Amy told her.

The gazebo was a round, open, little house with a peaked roof, built on a low platform. It stood between the two riding rings, so that onlookers could watch

the action from there without getting sunburned.

In the gazebo, a girl leaned back in one of the white chairs and stared straight ahead, waiting.

"Hillary," Cassie said.

Had she come to gloat because she'd gotten Majesty to ride, after all? Or was she here waiting for Trisha to make a final decision?

"She was already sitting in the gazebo when I got here," Amy said.

"Have you seen Trisha?" Cassie asked.

"I think she's in the barn," Amy said.

"Let's go talk to her," said Cassie. "I can't wait one second longer. I have to find out about Majesty!"

She and Amy hurried into the barn and up the alley between two rows of horse stalls. They passed Freckles—Amy fed him a carrot on her way by—and Charlie, Bliss, and Allegra.

Then Trisha stepped out of a stall at the end of a row, and spotted the two girls.

"Hi there," she called out. "I was just about to saddle up Majesty."

"Does this mean that I'll be riding him?" Cassie practically shrieked.

"I believe it's about time for your lesson, isn't it?" Trisha said, as though there had never been any question about it. "Let's get him saddled."

Even in the gloom of the stable, the Lipizzan seemed to glow. There was something almost magical about his gleaming white coat and his huge, intelligent brown eyes. Cassie wouldn't have been surprised if he had suddenly spoken to her, or maybe even sprouted wings!

While Cassie was helping tack Majesty up, Trisha told the girls a little about him.

"Sara is right about Lipizzans. At one time, all the Lipizzans in the world were at the Spanish Riding School in Vienna, Austria. They were used for a complicated kind of dressage," Trisha said. "Then, fifty years or so ago, during World War II, an American general brought some of those horses to the United States. A little later, more of them were imported. But there still aren't many Lipizzans here, so each one is quite special."

As Trisha held up the bridle, Majesty lowered his beautiful head so that she could slip it on.

"It looks as if he's bowing to his subjects," said Amy, bowing back and giggling.

"Who owned Majesty before you bought him?" Cassie asked Trisha, buckling the throatlatch on the bridle.

"A friend of mine did. She used him for jumping. But she retired from the horse-show circuit and felt that she just couldn't put in the time with Majesty that he needed. She knew I would give him a good home and plenty to do, so she sold him to me," said Trisha.

She had picked out a saddle pad and placed it gently on Majesty's broad back. Next came the saddle that Cassie used.

Cassie reached carefully under the horse for the girth and buckled it up.

Trisha fastened the breast collar across Majesty's broad chest and stood back.

"We're all set," she said. "I want you to ride Majesty in the indoor ring for fifteen or twenty minutes, Cassie. It will warm him up for jumping and also give you a chance to get used to each other."

Cassie still couldn't quite believe that she would be riding this magical horse. In her excitement, she forgot all about Hillary. She and Amy, and Trisha and Majesty walked down a side alley to the indoor ring. A few moments later, Cassie was in the saddle, looking down at the powerful white shoulders and strong neck of her new horse.

"You'll have to make some adjustments," Trisha told her. "Allegra is a slower horse, less quick to respond to your aids."

Trisha went on, "Majesty is bigger than Allegra, too. He'll feel rather different to you."

Cassie nodded. Even sitting still, she knew she was riding a much larger and stronger animal.

"Let's start out with some circles and figure eights," Trisha said, walking to the sideline. Amy was standing just outside the ring, watching through the fence.

Cassie felt a little nervous and jittery, but at the same time she was almost bursting with eagerness to try Majesty out. She nudged the white horse forward with her legs, first in a medium walk, and then in a trot. She could feel Majesty's powerful legs moving under her in perfect rhythm.

"Good, Cassie. Now the canter," Trisha said.

As Majesty moved into the "one-two-three" beat of the canter, Cassie relaxed in the center of the saddle. She was thrilled with this new horse! Other students would also ride Majesty at Birchwood, but none could love him as much as she already did.

Suddenly, there was a loud bang from somewhere inside the stable. Startled, Majesty shied away from the noise, jumping to one side. It all happened so quickly, and Majesty was so strong, that Cassie's feet were jerked out of the stirrups. She slipped sideways in the saddle. If she hadn't grabbed hold of Majesty's mane, she would have fallen off.

Then Trisha was at their side, her hand on the

headstall of the bridle to steady Majesty. As she spoke soothingly to him, the horse pranced nervously in place for a few seconds. Then he calmed down, although his eyes and ears were still focused on the door that led into the stall area.

Once Cassie had gotten herself settled in the saddle again, Trisha called out, "What *was* that?"

Amy was peering through the door toward the rows of stalls, her back toward the ring. At the sound of Trisha's voice, she turned to answer.

But before she could say anything, Hillary appeared in the doorway. "Sorry," she said. "There was a metal bucket in the alley, and I stumbled over it."

Cassie could see Amy shaking her head. Did she mean that Hillary had kicked the metal bucket on purpose?

"Please be careful. We're having a lesson in here," Trisha said sternly to Hillary. To Cassie, she added, "Ride Majesty around for a few more minutes, and then we'll go outside and try some jumps."

Cassie had learned to jump in stages. She had begun by riding Allegra over a single pole lying on the ground between two uprights, first in a walk and then in a trot. Next, Trisha had added two crossed poles behind the single pole. Cassie learned to jump that at a trot.

She moved on from two small jumps in a row, still made of crossed poles, and still riding Allegra in a trot; to jumping them in a canter; to several different kinds of low fences in a canter. Now she was jumping two-and-a-half-foot fences on Allegra.

For Majesty, Trisha started Cassie out with four two-foot fences in a large oval. As they took off over the first fence, Cassie realized that jumping on Majesty would be a whole new experience.

She remembered to do all of the things that a rider should do, such as leaning her upper body forward as Majesty gathered himself to jump. She looked straight ahead, and her weight stayed in the middle of the saddle. Her legs were steady against the girth. Her back remained flat. And Majesty did the rest.

Cassie had a feeling that the strong white horse could have easily cleared jumps two times higher than this one without straining. He seemed to hang in the air for several seconds before landing smoothly on the far side. Then he went sailing over the second jump. And the third and fourth.

Allegra had been fun to jump on. But jumping on Majesty was the most exciting thing Cassie had ever done in her life.

They moved smoothly around the course a second time.

"Well done, Cassie," Trisha said. "Why don't you walk him for the rest of your hour?"

Cassie was sure that Majesty could have jumped for another hour. The horse wasn't even sweaty.

Amy had been sitting alone in the gazebo, watching Cassie put Majesty through his paces. She met her friend at the gate to the outdoor ring when the lesson was over.

"Hillary kicked that metal bucket on purpose, I'm sure of it," Amy said to Hillary as they walked back to the barn. "She was hoping to cause problems between you and Majesty."

"Well, we'd never be able to prove it. And even if we could, Trisha hates tattling," Cassie said. "Maybe now that Hillary's seen what a great team Majesty and I make, she'll get her mind on something else."

The Missing Hat

Cassie didn't think about Hillary much that week. She thought mostly about Majesty, and how exciting it would be to jump on him at horse shows, and maybe even win.

She also wondered who else would be riding Majesty. All of the horses at Birchwood were shared among the students. It had never bothered Cassie that a younger boy and girl rode Allegra, too. But she had to admit to herself that she wished Majesty were hers alone to ride.

The next Saturday morning, her mom drove her to the barn half an hour early. First Cassie stopped by Majesty's stall. She wanted the horse to learn to

38

recognize her right away, so she'd brought him some fresh carrots and apple slices as a treat.

She laid her riding hat on the shelf outside Majesty's stall door and took the snacks out of a plastic bag. The white horse accepted them gently and politely. He didn't snatch or gobble like Freckles. Majesty plucked each carrot and apple slice neatly from Cassie's hand with his velvety upper lip. Then he bobbed his head up and down as he chewed, and Cassie could tell he was enjoying them.

When she had run out of carrots and apples, she walked outside to watch two of the older riders taking their horses over some high jumps. Every time one of the girls cleared a four-foot fence, Cassie imagined herself on Majesty doing exactly the same thing in the not-so-distant future.

Then Amy's dad dropped Amy off. When she and Cassie walked into the barn together to start tacking up their horses, Hillary was already there, saddling Bliss with Robert.

"Hey, Hillary," Cassie said casually.

Hillary barely nodded before she led Bliss down the alley toward the indoor ring.

"We'd better hurry," Amy said to Cassie as Robert helped them finish saddling Majesty and Freckles. "Sara's saddle is gone. She's already in the ring."

Trisha didn't like them to be late to a lesson. And if a student was too late, Trisha would start the lesson without her.

"I'll catch up with you. I just have to grab my hat," Cassie said.

Cassie led Majesty out of his stall and reached out for her riding hat, but the hat wasn't on the shelf.

Cassie was stunned. She was absolutely certain that she had placed it on the shelf outside Majesty's stall door. But it was nowhere to be seen. And she couldn't ride without her hat. It wouldn't be safe.

"The hat didn't just walk away," she said to herself. "Maybe it fell off the shelf and rolled out of sight."

Cassie led Majesty back into his stall and latched the door. She looked around on the floor of the stall. But the hat wasn't there.

Then she looked up and down the alley. No hat.

Cassie heard Trisha calling her name: "Cassie, we're waiting."

"I'll be right there!" Cassie called back.

She searched feverishly over, under, and behind everything at that end of the stable.

Finally, Cassie uncovered her riding hat in a pile of dirty straw, soon to be carried off to the trash by Robert.

How had it gotten there?!

Cassie barely had a moment to brush some of the straw off and jam the hat down on her head. She raced back to Majesty's stall and led the horse to the indoor ring in a brisk trot.

By this time, Cassie was out of breath and totally frazzled. And for the first few minutes of the group lesson, she didn't look like much of a rider. In fact, she wasn't even sitting in the saddle very well. "Stop slouching. Line up your ear, shoulder, hip, and ankle!" she repeated crossly to herself.

Cassie's mind was still on her hat, buried in the pile of dirty straw. Who had hidden it there?

"As if it could have been anyone other than Hillary," she thought in disgust. Hillary probably hoped to prove to Trisha that Cassie and Majesty weren't a good match. Well, she wasn't going to give Hillary the satisfaction of seeing her plans work. Cassie was *not* going to mess up with Majesty, no matter what Hillary tried.

When Trisha said, "Cassie, show us what you and Majesty can do," Cassie gave orders to herself. "Get your mind on your business! Straight line from elbow to hand to rein to mouth. Feel the horse under you."

Cassie knew that her riding style would change now that she was riding Majesty. For starters, the white horse was used to being ridden on a much shorter rein than Allegra. Cassie was always in close contact with his mouth through her hands on the reins. His body was more tightly gathered together, too. And his movements were shorter and higher, almost like prancing.

For the first time in her life, Cassie felt as though she was riding a real show horse, even though all she was really doing was going through her exercises in the indoor ring. Thoughts of Hillary faded, and she was aware of nothing but the big horse beneath her.

Cassie's face must have shown everyone how pleased she was. As she and Majesty walked to their place near the gate, Hillary rode past them for her turn in the ring. And she gave Cassie such a dirty look that Cassie's heart sank.

Cassie wanted to be able to focus her thoughts on the most important thing while she was at Birchwood—improving her riding. She didn't want to have to waste time worrying about what Hillary might do next.

"I guess I don't have a choice. I have to talk to Trisha about Hillary," Cassie said to herself. "And I might as well get it over with." As soon as class was finished, she asked Trisha if she could speak with her privately.

Amy raised her eyebrows. And Hillary frowned.

"Of course you can," Trisha said. "As soon as you've unsaddled, Cassie, come to my office."

"What's this all about?" Amy whispered to her outside the tack room.

"Tell you later," Cassie whispered back, because she could see that Hillary was listening.

In Trisha's office, Cassie told Trisha what Amy had said about Hillary and the metal bucket. Then she told her about her riding hat disappearing from the shelf.

"Hillary's angry with me about Majesty," Cassie said. "I think maybe she's trying to play tricks so that Majesty and I don't work out."

"Hillary isn't right for Majesty," Trisha said straight off, which cheered Cassie up immediately. "Majesty needs a gentle touch, and Hillary sometimes rides heavily on the reins. And sometimes she leans heavily on people, too," Trisha added. "As to the hat, I agree it does look suspicious, but you have no real proof that it was Hillary, do you?"

Cassie was forced to shake her head. "But it had to have been Hillary. None of my friends would play such a nasty trick on me."

Trisha nodded sympathetically. "I know Hillary can be difficult, Cassie. On the other hand, she isn't having an easy time of it herself."

"You mean, moving here from California?" Cassie said, remembering her talk with her parents.

"Yes, that," said Trisha, "and the fact of having a stepfather whom she still doesn't feel certain about, and . . ."

"Mr. Craig isn't Hillary's dad?" Cassie said, shocked.

She'd thought that Hillary's real reason for riding was to be just like her father.

"No, Hillary's father died when Hillary was quite young. Mrs. Craig remarried a year ago," said Trisha. "I don't approve of gossiping, but I'm telling you this to help you understand some of the reasons that Hillary sometimes acts the way she does."

"Did her real father ride, too?" Cassie asked, recalling Hillary's announcement that she had been riding since she was an infant.

But Trisha was shaking her head. "Hillary started riding three years ago. And she rides remarkably well for just three years." Trisha smiled at Cassie. "Almost as well as you do," she said.

"Do you think Hillary *likes* riding?" Cassie asked. "She sure doesn't seem to like the group."

"Hillary's in the group because her mother wants her to make friends," Trisha explained.

Cassie rolled her eyes. That certainly wasn't working out!

"As far as liking riding—it's a good question," said Trisha. "Hillary's good at it. But I don't know if she likes it, or if she's doing it because she thinks it will please her stepfather, especially if she wins."

"And if Hillary wins at horse shows, she thinks her stepfather will like her more?" Cassie said.

"Probably," said Trisha.

Trisha nodded. "Now you understand what I mean about Hillary's worries," she said. "Not that I'm excusing bad behavior on Hillary's part," Trisha added. "And if you ever feel that she's doing anything to cause you difficulties on purpose, I'd appreciate it if . . ."

Suddenly, the door to Trisha's office burst open. It was Hillary, her face beet red. "I know what Cassie's been saying. And I didn't hide her stupid hat in the straw!" Hillary yelled at Trisha. She was so worked up that she threw her own hat on the floor. "Cassie's just trying to get me into trouble!"

"No one has said anything about straw," Trisha replied calmly.

"No? But . . . ," Hillary fumbled, realizing she'd made a mistake.

How could she have known about the pile of straw, if she hadn't hidden the hat herself?

"Cassie is jealous of me because I ride better than she does!" Hillary said.

Which was so unfair that Cassie couldn't think of an answer.

But she didn't have to, because Trisha said, "Hillary, this has gone far enough. I'm not used to having pointless and unpleasant scenes at Birchwood." Then she added, "And I *won't* have them. Please ask your mother or father to get in touch with me."

When Trisha mentioned her parents, Hillary's face faded from red to white. "But I . . . ," she began rather weakly.

"As soon as possible," Trisha said firmly.

Hillary backed out of the office so quickly that she left her hat behind, on the floor.

Trisha shook her head. "I'm afraid that Hillary isn't going to be much help when it comes to reducing the tension around here," she said. She looked at Cassie for a moment, and went on. "Maybe you could try to get on better terms with her. Would you do that for me?"

"How?" Cassie asked, wishing she never had to deal with Hillary Craig again.

"That's a hard one," Trisha said. Then her gaze fell on Hillary's riding hat, which had rolled under her desk. "Here," she said, handing Cassie the hat. "Maybe you could return this to Hillary on your way home.

Show her you want to be friends. Or, at the very least, not enemies."

Cassie took the riding hat. "I'll try," she said, willing to try it for Trisha.

But Cassie didn't have any great hopes. And she didn't think Trisha did, either.

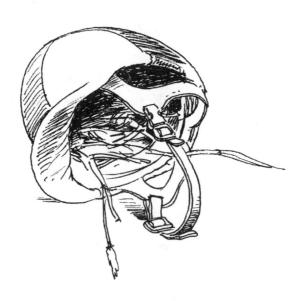

A Wonderful Surprise

Trisha gave Cassie Hillary's address on Lilac Drive, a street in a brand-new subdivision not far from the stable.

When Cassie's mom drove up to the curb in front of 22 Lilac Drive, both Cassie and Amy gasped. It was a huge, two-story brick house, with big columns across the front, a circular driveway, and a tennis court to one side.

"That's the biggest house I've ever seen," Cassie said.

The Craigs' house was also brand-new, so new that it was hard to believe anyone had moved in yet. The emerald-green lawn was perfect. There were no

bikes, or skates, or toys to be seen.

"It looks like a public library," Amy added, "but without any people."

"Are you sure this is the right address?" Mrs. Sinclair asked Cassie. "It does look empty. Or maybe the Craigs just haven't had time to add any personal touches."

"It's the number Trisha wrote down," Cassie said, rechecking her slip of paper.

"Well, go ahead, honey," her mom said.

"Want to come with me?" Cassie said to Amy.

"Uh-uh. I'll wait in the car with your mom," said Amy.

Cassie walked toward the front door, with Hillary's riding hat under her arm. Her feet moved slower and slower as she got closer. She climbed the steps between the giant columns and rang the front doorbell.

Cassie could hear chimes echoing inside the house, but no one came to the door. She was just about to leave when the door finally swung open.

And there was Hillary, taken completely by surprise to find Cassie standing on her front steps.

"Hi," Cassie said.

"Hi," said Hillary, staring past her at Mrs. Sinclair's car, with Amy peering out the back window.

"I'm on my way home from the stable. Trisha asked me to bring your riding hat," Cassie explained, holding it out to her.

"Thanks," Hillary said, taking the hat without inviting Cassie inside.

Behind Hillary, a large glass-fronted cabinet covered one wall of an entry hall. Inside it, Cassie could see the gleam of gold and silver trophies.

"Wow!" Cassie exclaimed.

The trophies seemed to pull her forward. Without thinking, Cassie stepped around Hillary and into the entry hall to take a closer look.

The cabinet held at least twenty large trophies decorated with horses, plus a handful of smaller ones, and many colored ribbons.

"Did you win these at horse shows?" Cassie asked Hillary, feeling very outclassed.

Hillary answered, "Some of them are mine. But most are my stepfather's."

Now Cassie was close enough to read the dates on the trophies and ribbons. Many were fifteen years old or more.

"I have an important engagement to get ready for," Hillary said in her snobbiest voice. "Thanks for stopping by to bring me my hat."

Cassie shrugged. "Sure."

She couldn't think of anything more to say to Hillary, anyway. She'd done what Trisha had asked her to do, and it hadn't made a bit of difference.

But as Cassie turned to leave, she heard voices at the back of the house. Then, "Hillary?" a man called out.

"In here," Hillary replied.

A small, thin man with curly, dark hair stepped into the entry hall. "Oh, you have a friend with you," he said briskly.

"Dad, I've told you about Cassie," Hillary said.

"I'll bet you have!" Cassie thought to herself.

"Nice to meet you, Cassie," said Mr. Craig, shaking her hand. Then to Hillary he added, "Lunch will be ready in a few minutes."

Hillary nodded. "I'll be right there."

Mr. Craig smiled at Cassie. "Are you keeping Hillary company for lunch?" he asked.

"No, thank you, I can't," Cassie said. "My mom is waiting for me. Goodbye."

She slipped out the front door and hurried down the walk toward the car, still shivering a little from the Craigs' air-conditioning. Cassie found herself actually feeling sorry for Hillary. Hillary had looked pretty lonesome in the huge house.

Cassie and her mom dropped Amy off at her house. Then they joined Mr. Sinclair for a quick lunch of chicken salad sandwiches at their kitchen table.

When lunch was over and they'd put their dishes in the dishwasher, Cassie's dad said, "Your mom and I would like to take you for a short ride in the car."

"But I planned to bike over to Amy's this afternoon," Cassie said. After all, she and Amy hadn't had time to really discuss her visit to Hillary's house.

"This won't take too long," said Mrs. Sinclair. "And I think you'll find it interesting."

"Okay," Cassie said. "Maybe you can drop me off at the Lins' on the way home."

They got into her dad's car and drove here and there for fifteen minutes or so, until Cassie finally said, "Dad, where *are* we going?" Her mom said, "Bill, don't tease her."

Her father grinned, made a couple of right turns, and ended up on Middle Road, the same road that Birchwood Stable was on.

"We're going to drive right past Birchwood," Cassie pointed out.

But they didn't drive past the stable. Her dad turned into the lane and kept going until he reached the barn.

"Why are we here?" Cassie asked, more puzzled than ever.

"We wanted to check out our investment," Mr. Sinclair replied, opening his car door.

"What does he mean?" Cassie asked her mother, as the two of them climbed out of the car.

"He means Majesty," her mother said with a big smile.

"We've leased him for you, Cassie," her father added.

Cassie couldn't take in what they were saying for a moment. "You've leased . . . ," she began, and stopped. "Majesty is all mine to ride?" she shrieked, understanding at last.

"All yours, sweetie," said her dad. "I spoke to Trisha Prescott about it on the phone this morning, and she's preparing a contract for us to sign."

Cassie thought she would burst with happiness. If her parents had leased Majesty, she wouldn't have to share him with anyone else at the stable. Plus, she could ride him every day if she wanted!

But first she had to ask, "Can we afford it?"

"Yes, because I'm working on a big, new project," her mother said. Mrs. Sinclair was a technical writer for a computer company.

"And we'll take a cheaper vacation," said Mr.

Sinclair. "So, let's go see this remarkable animal."

"Oh, yes!" cried Cassie, eagerly.

"Before we do, we have to stop by Ms. Prescott's office to sign that contract," Mrs. Sinclair reminded them.

CHAPTER
SIX

Hillary in Hot Water

But Trisha's car wasn't parked outside the barn. Robert was leading Freckles and Charlie back to the paddock. After he said hello to Cassie and her parents, he added, "If you're looking for Trisha, she's teaching a class in Milford. She should be here in the next half-hour or so."

Cassie took her parents to the barn instead. "In the meantime, I'll show you Majesty," she told them.

The three of them walked up to the alley toward the Lipizzan's stall.

"Majesty?" Cassie called out, expecting the big white horse to poke his head out over the stall door. But he didn't.

57

"He's probably taking a catnap," Cassie said.

"Don't you mean a horse nap?" her dad joked.

When they peered over the door, Cassie was surprised to discover that the stall was empty.

"Maybe he's out in the paddock," Cassie told her parents, a little uneasily. Now that Majesty's was hers alone to ride, Cassie wanted to know where he was every second of every day.

"Robert?" Cassie called out.

"I'm in the tack room," Robert called back. He stepped into the alley to talk to Cassie.

"Where's Majesty?" she asked.

"Oh, he's in one of the outdoor rings," Robert said.

"An outdoor ring?" Cassie repeated. "Why?"

Trisha never turned the stable horses loose in an outdoor ring for exercise, because jumps were usually set up there. The horses might get tangled up in the jumps and hurt themselves. Outdoor rings were for riding only. Did that mean someone was riding Majesty?

Robert answered Cassie before she even asked. "That Craig girl is riding him."

"What?" Cassie said. How could that be? Majesty was hers now.

Mr. Sinclair placed his hand on Cassie's shoulder to calm her. "There must be some mistake. We've leased Majesty for Cassie. I spoke to Ms. Prescott about it only a few hours ago. No one else should be riding him."

Robert shrugged and shook his head. "I guess Trisha forgot to mention it to me," he said. "Hillary and her father drove here about forty-five minutes ago. And when I told them that Trisha wasn't around, Mr. Craig insisted that Hillary try out the Lipizzan. He wouldn't take no for an answer."

"I made it clear to Mr. Craig that he would have to square it with Trisha when she got back. He said there wouldn't be a problem, that Hillary had talked to Trisha and had gotten her approval," Robert ended.

Cassie found it hard to concentrate on what Robert was saying. She was too angry to listen to much more than the words pounding in her own head: "Hillary Craig is riding my horse!"

She stormed out of the barn, while her mother called out after her, "Wait, Cassie, I'm sure there's been a misunderstanding."

"There's no misunderstanding," Cassie muttered to herself as she marched toward the outdoor rings. "Hillary knew Trisha would be away all afternoon, giving her the perfect opportunity to ride Majesty. She'll do anything to ride him, including lie!"

Mr. Craig wasn't sitting in the gazebo like a visitor,

watching Hillary ride from a distance. Cassie heard him talking from inside the far ring, giving Hillary advice from close-up.

Cassie saw Hillary's dark-brown riding hat bobbing up and down above the tall fence as she cantered across the outdoor ring. Hillary and Majesty were headed toward the line of jumps.

"Stop!" Cassie shouted.

Hillary didn't seem to hear. She was focused on the jumps in front of her.

"Don't squeeze him with your legs, Hillary," Mr. Craig called out to his stepdaughter. "Look straight in front of you."

Cassie started to run toward the gate of the ring where Hillary was riding.

Mr. Craig was still giving instructions. "Let the reins move with his head. Your legs are behind the stirrups, get them under you."

As angry as Cassie was, she wondered, "How can Hillary possibly manage to follow all of those orders while she's trying to ride a strange horse over a jump?"

Cassie unlatched the gate to the outdoor ring and shoved it open in time to see Hillary and Majesty sail over the last jump.

On the far side of the jump, Hillary pulled Majesty

up hard, pinching his mouth. His ears flattened with annoyance as he felt the pinch.

Cassie shouted at the top of her lungs, "Hillary Craig, get off my horse!"

Mr. Craig was standing near the fence at one side of the ring, still watching Hillary. But when Cassie shouted, he turned quickly around.

"Why, it's Cassie, isn't it? What do you mean, *your* horse?" He sounded truly surprised.

Majesty is my horse now. My parents leased him for me," Cassie said.

Mr. Sinclair hurried through the gate. "That's right. We leased the Lipizzan for Cassie this morning," he said to Mr. Craig. "Hello, I'm Bill Sinclair."

"Andrew Craig." Mr. Craig shook hands with Cassie's dad. "Did you speak to Ms. Prescott about the horse?"

"Absolutely," said Mr. Sinclair. "I made the arrangements by phone. My wife and I are here now to sign the contract."

"I'm sorry," said Mr. Craig. "There must have been some confusion between Ms. Prescott and Hillary."

Instead of riding Majesty back to the group at the gate, Hillary had steered him toward the back fence. She was bent over, pretending to look at her right stirrup.

"Hillary!" Mr. Craig called out.

"Yes?" she called back, as though she had no idea what might be going on, with Cassie and her dad standing right there.

Mr. Craig waved his arm to let Hillary know he wanted her at the gate.

Hillary pulled Majesty to a stop behind Mr. Craig and slid down from the saddle.

"Cassie tells me that this is her horse," Mr. Craig said.

"Since when?" Hillary was dumbstruck.

"Since this morning," Cassie replied, looking Hillary straight in the eye. "That's when my parents leased him for me."

Hillary scowled, and her face turned dark red.

"When did you speak to Ms. Prescott about riding Majesty?" Mr. Craig asked.

"Why, right after our lesson, I think," Hillary mumbled.

"No, you didn't," Cassie said. "I was in Trisha's office right after our lesson, remember?"

"So that's that, Hillary," said Mr. Craig. "We'll just find you another horse. I don't know how you got the idea that this one was available."

Cassie saw Trisha coming toward them. Mrs. Sinclair was right behind her.

"I want to know exactly what is going on here," Trisha said, as she joined them near the gate. "Hillary, you did not have permission to ride Majesty, even if the Sinclairs hadn't leased him. I have been looking for a horse for you. And I will continue to do so, if you can convince me that you're the kind of student that I want to have at Birchwood Stable. You will have to change your attitude, though."

Mr. Craig said, "Ms. Prescott, I'm sure Hillary meant no harm."

Trisha said, "Hillary, hand Cassie the reins, please."

Hillary thrust Majesty's reins in Cassie's direction, her gaze fixed on the ground.

"Let's talk about this in my office," Trisha said to Mr. Craig. "I'll meet you there in a few minutes."

Hillary hurried away, in the direction of the barn.

Mr. Craig turned to Cassie's parents. "I'm sorry about all of this," he told them.

When Mr. Craig had left, Cassie rested her cheek against Majesty's warm neck. She closed her eyes and imagined herself on Majesty, sailing over the jumps at the first horse show.

Trisha smiled warmly at Mr. and Mrs. Sinclair. "So what do you think of Cassie's horse?"

"He's just beautiful!" Mrs. Sinclair exclaimed, standing back a little. She was a bit leery of horses.

"He's one powerful-looking fellow," said Mr. Sinclair. "Cassie, can you really handle this horse?"

"Would you like to show your parents how well the two of you work together?" Trisha said to Cassie.

"I'd love to!" Cassie said.

She was still wearing her riding breeches and boots. And Trisha had brought out a hat to lend her.

While her parents sat in the gazebo and watched, Cassie put Majesty through his paces in one of the outdoor rings. Once he was warmed up, she jumped a few fences for them, too.

Her parents and Trisha clapped as she and Majesty cleared the last fence with a couple of feet to spare.

Cassie pulled in her Lipizzan and thought, "This is turning out to be one of the best days of my life!"

Hillary's Horse

Cassie planned to ride Majesty at least a couple of hours every day. "I want to be sure that you're getting your money's worth," she said to her parents.

"So you're doing it for us, not for yourself. Is that what you're telling me?" her dad joked.

And her mom said, "Two hours a day in the summertime is one thing, Cassie. But when school starts, you may have to cut back."

"Even more reason for me to get in as much riding as I can now," Cassie said.

There were also some local horse shows coming up. The show at Barker Farm was only three weeks away, and Cassie needed to practice, practice, practice. She hoped she wasn't thinking like Hillary, but she did want her parents to feel that they weren't wasting their money leasing Majesty for her. A trophy or a ribbon would be nice!

Cassie preferred to ride in the morning, before the sun got too hot, and before the riding rings were too crowded. All of the Birchwood horses were fed around seven o'clock every morning. Cassie would get to the stable, ready to saddle up, before nine. Since Trisha didn't schedule any classes before ten, Cassie and Majesty usually had an hour to themselves.

But on Thursday that first week, Cassie rolled up to the barn on her bike to discover quite a crowd already on hand. Besides Trisha's blue truck and trailer in the parking area, there was a green station wagon and a white horse van with "Herricks' Horse Farm" painted on the side. Tied to a hook on the back of the van, a stocky bay horse was switching flies with his tail. He whinnied at Cassie in a friendly way as she walked past.

A couple of men in jeans were sitting on hay bales just inside the barn, talking to Robert Martin. And as Cassie headed down the alley toward Majesty's stall, she heard more voices coming from the indoor ring. She recognized Trisha's voice, and another voice sounded a lot like Hillary.

What would Hillary be doing at the stable so early on a Thursday morning? Curious, Cassie turned around and walked toward the ring to take a look.

The first thing Cassie saw when she stepped through the door was a striking chestnut horse with two white feet and a blaze on its face. Then she checked out the rider: It was Hillary, looking excited, and maybe a bit nervous, too.

Trisha was standing beside the horse. Cassie could hear her talking to Mr. and Mrs. Craig, who were outside the fence.

"I personally think he's a little too much horse for Hillary," Trisha was saying to them. "He's a Thoroughbred, he's high-strung. I think she would do much better leasing the bay. He's steadier, he's used to young riders, he's been to many horse shows and has done well at them."

Mr. Craig shook his head. "I disagree. Hillary's an excellent rider. She needs an excellent horse, and the Thoroughbred's just the ticket. What do you say, Hillary?"

Hillary shrugged. "I don't know. I like him, but I really want a Lipizzan." Her lower lip jutted out as she pouted.

"I couldn't find another Lipizzan on such short

notice," Trisha said. "The bay is a fine horse. I recommend that you lease it for Hillary."

"The bay is a horse for a five-year-old," Mr. Craig scoffed. "Hillary won't win any ribbons on a tame horse like that."

Trisha rubbed her forehead as if she had a headache. "That's not so, Mr. Craig. The bay has brought in his share of ribbons. Why not let Hillary try him out next?"

Hillary took her father's side. "The bay looks as if he should be pulling a farm wagon! And he plods—I won't win anything on him. If I can't have a Lipizzan, I want the Thoroughbred." She appealed to her mother: "Mom!"

"Hillary, you know that I know nothing whatsoever about horses," her mother said.

"Maybe neither horse is quite right for Hillary," Trisha suggested. "Why don't I talk to a few more people, and . . ."

Hillary might have gone along with Trisha's suggestion if she hadn't caught sight of Cassie just then. Seeing Cassie—and perhaps thinking about Majesty—seemed to make her twice as determined to lease the Thoroughbred.

"No!" Hillary said, shaking her head. "I want this horse. The horse shows start soon, and Thor and I are going to make a great team and beat everybody. I'm sure of it!" She stared straight at Cassie as she said it.

Trisha looked at Mr. Craig.

He grinned and patted Hillary on the back. "Now you're talking. You've made me very proud, Hillary. You have winning in your blood, same as I have."

Hillary glanced at Cassie again and smiled smugly. "Thor and I will be blue-ribbon winners, I know we will."

"Would you like to ride Thor around some more, Hillary?" her mother asked. "We can come back for you."

"No, I'll ride him on Saturday at my group lesson," Hillary said. "Wait for me, okay?"

Hillary hurriedly slipped out of the saddle. "I'll put him in his stall now," she said, reins in hand. "Which stall will be his, Trisha?"

"I think the one across from Majesty would be fine," Trisha said.

"Great," said Hillary. "I'll unsaddle him and get him settled."

That was the first time Cassie had ever heard Hillary volunteer for any work herself. And it probably had a lot more to do with showing off her new horse to Cassie than helping out Trisha.

Trisha said, "Thank you, Hillary. Mr. and Mrs.

Craig, we can sign the contract in my office."

Cassie was standing in Majesty's stall, grooming him with a dandy brush, when Hillary led her new horse to the stall opposite.

"Oh, hello," Hillary said brightly, as though she had just noticed Cassie for the first time that day. "Have you seen my horse? His name is Thor."

"He's a beauty," Cassie said, continuing to brush Majesty.

Cassie had promised her parents—and herself— that she wouldn't waste any more time getting angry about Hillary Craig. After all, Majesty now was hers alone.

"Yes, he's gorgeous," Hillary said. "And the best thing about him is that since he's leased, I can ride whenever I want. I can ride him every day, if I feel like it." Hillary fiddled with Thor's mane with a curry comb.

Then she must have remembered that Cassie could ride Majesty whenever she wanted, too. She tossed the curry comb aside and stamped out of Thor's stall and up the alley.

By the time Saturday morning rolled around, Cassie and the Lipizzan were really getting to know each other. She had learned some of his funny little habits, like the way he stretched his neck out and sniffed her as she stepped through the stall door. Once Majesty was certain it was Cassie, he nickered a greeting deep in his throat.

Or the way he rubbed his forehead up and down on her shoulder after she pulled his bridle off. And the way he hated the sound of the fly-spray can. He always turned his ears straight back and stamped one foot as if to say, "Not in this stall!"

When they were in the ring, Majesty would let Cassie know when she was doing something that bothered him: either leaning too far forward in the saddle, or sitting a bit crooked, or pushing him off balance. The horse would curve his neck slightly, so one eye could peer in her direction. Cassie could almost hear him saying, "Hey! What's going on up there?"

Cassie figured Majesty had a right to ask. After all, he was the one with more experience. She had a lot more to learn from him than he did from her.

Cassie had already come to depend on the Lipizzan's intelligence and on his excellent attitude. Majesty went out of his way to do what she asked, from small things, like trotting slower or faster, to much bigger things, like jumping a three-foot fence.

Cassie couldn't have been happier than she was with the beautiful white horse.

But as soon as she saw Hillary on Saturday, she knew that things weren't going at all well for her and Thor.

Cassie had spent Friday night at Amy's. Mr. Lin drove them to Birchwood about half an hour before their Saturday group lesson. Cassie wanted to spend some time with Majesty in his stall. And she wanted him to get to know Amy, too.

Amy had come prepared with enough apple slices and carrots to feed Majesty and Freckles and three or four more horses. But on their way into the barn, Cassie and Amy happened to glance toward the outdoor rings. In the farther one, they saw a girl with reddish-brown hair riding a chestnut horse.

"It's Hillary on her new horse, Thor," Cassie said to Amy.

"Well, I don't think they're having any fun," Amy said.

Thor's head was raised high in the air, and Hillary was really bouncing around in the saddle.

"It looks as if they're having problems," Cassie agreed.

"Let's watch!" said Amy.

"Maybe we shouldn't," Cassie said. An audience was probably the last thing Hillary wanted right now.

"*She* watches *you*," Amy pointed out. "Come on."

So Cassie followed Amy over to the gazebo, and they sat down.

By this time, not only was Thor high-headed, he was dancing around. The more Hillary tugged on the reins, the more he fought the bit.

"She should loosen up on his mouth," Cassie said, remembering what Trisha had told her about Hillary's heavy hands on the reins. "He would stop fighting her then."

"I think she's scared of him," Amy said, adding, "That's a tall horse. Hillary has an awfully long way to fall."

Hillary did look panicky. And suddenly, to make matters worse, Thor lunged forward. Now he was trying to take the bit away from Hillary altogether.

Cassie didn't know what would have happened if an older girl, Jane Clark, hadn't ridden into the ring at that point. She took one look at what was going on between Hillary and Thor and moved her horse forward. She pressed Thor toward the fence, so he'd have to stop jumping around.

"Loosen up on the reins," Jane yelled to Hillary at the same time.

In a few seconds, Thor was standing still. Jane jumped off her horse and grabbed Thor's bridle so that Hillary could climb down.

When her feet touched the ground, Hillary almost collapsed. She really had been frightened.

"Let's leave before Hillary sees us," Cassie said to Amy. She was feeling sorry for the girl again. "There's no sense in making her more upset than she already is."

Where Is Hillary?

Hillary was mounted on Thor and ready to ride in the indoor ring when the group class began fifteen minutes later. She was brave. Cassie had to give her that.

Amy put it a different way, though. "I'd call it hard-headed and just plain dumb," Amy whispered to Cassie. "I'd never get on that horse again if I were Hillary!"

Whatever it was, Hillary took her turn in the middle of the ring, just like everyone else. Cassie and Amy knew that Thor had frightened her badly, but Hillary didn't say anything to Trisha about it. She squared her shoulders and started putting Thor through his paces as though she felt totally comfortable with him.

Of course, Trisha helped out by insisting that Hillary slow the horse down. "Keep him calm," Trisha told her. "Thor might get excitable if he gets too warmed up."

"'Excitable'?" Amy whispered to Cassie as they watched from the gate. "That's putting it mildly!"

"Maybe he'll behave himself if Hillary keeps him under control from the start," Cassie whispered back.

But she found herself holding her breath during most of Hillary's ride. For Cassie, Thor was a little like a firecracker with a long fuse. It might take a while, but it was almost certainly going to go off!

"Slow down, Hillary . . . halt," Trisha finally called out from the sidelines. "Good work."

Cassie saw Hillary's shoulders slump as she rode Thor toward the group at the gate. She'd been holding herself so tensely that her shoulders had been up around her ears.

"He's a beautiful horse," Sara said shyly to Hillary once she'd joined them. After all, Sara hadn't witnessed the commotion in the outdoor ring.

"Thanks," Hillary mumbled, her thoughts elsewhere. Then she snapped out of it and added quickly, "Isn't he great?" Looking over at Cassie on

Majesty, Hillary said, "Thor's the handsomest horse around and a registered Thoroughbred, too."

Of course, Hillary didn't realize that Cassie had seen her earlier struggle. And she was not going to admit that Thor was anything but super, especially not with Cassie and Majesty getting along so well.

Cassie took her turn next. She could hear Trisha talking to the others while she and Majesty moved around the ring.

"It's very important always to keep in contact with your horse's mouth and to keep the same *light* contact, no matter if he's walking, trotting, or cantering—or even jumping," Trisha was saying. "See how Cassie's arms follow the movements of Majesty's head? As his head moves up and down, so do her arms. She stays balanced in the middle of the saddle, and her hands keep in light contact with his mouth through the reins."

Cassie and the Lipizzan walked, trotted, and cantered in smaller and smaller circles to the right, and then to the left. Cassie used half-halts—almost invisible signals to the horse through her legs and hands—to let him know they would be shifting gears to a faster or slower speed. Majesty was so smooth that Cassie often felt as if she were riding in a dream.

When Cassie and Majesty had stopped and backed

up, ready to take their place beside the gate, Trisha said, "Well done, Cassie. You're getting better and better."

"Being able to ride as often as I like is making a big difference," Cassie said happily. "And Majesty teaches me something every time I get on him."

Then Trisha said to the class, "Think of your contact with your horse's mouth as a steady, warm handshake. Keep your fingers closed firmly around the reins, with your thumbs on top and pressing down. And keep your elbows relaxed, so you can go with the horse's motion." She added, "The worst thing you can do is loosen up on the reins, letting the horse go faster and faster until he gets away from you, then panic and yank on him."

Cassie glanced at Hillary. Trisha was describing exactly what had happened between Hillary and Thor in the outdoor ring.

Hillary must have realized it, too. She was concentrating so hard on what Trisha was saying that her lips moved as she repeated it to herself.

"Okay, that's all for today," Trisha said. "I'll see all of you next Saturday for our group lesson. I want everyone to start thinking about our first horse show, at Barker Farm in Port Pleasant. It's only three weeks away. And Cassie and Hillary: I'll see you tomorrow

afternoon at the usual time for your jumping classes."

"I can't wait to take Thor over the three-footers," Hillary said brightly.

"I think we'll start with some lower jumps first," Trisha said with a smile.

"I'm just glad I won't have to watch it," Amy whispered to Cassie. "I have a feeling that Hillary's going to be flying through the air without her horse!"

When Cassie arrived for her lesson the next day, she expected to find Hillary already hanging around the outdoor ring, waiting to see how well Cassie and Majesty were doing. Or waiting to catch Cassie messing up, which is how Amy would have put it.

But Hillary was nowhere in sight. And Cassie didn't mess up. She and Majesty sailed over every jump so beautifully that Trisha actually clapped!

Cassie was so caught up in her riding that she didn't give Hillary another thought until her class was over, and Trisha said, "I wonder where Hillary is. She should have been warming Thor up."

And suddenly Robert called from the barn, "Trisha! It's Mrs. Craig on the phone."

As Trisha hurried to take the call, Cassie led Majesty to the barn. Walking him toward his stall, Cassie paused when she overheard Trisha saying, "I'm sorry to hear that." Trisha went on, "I know that a stomach flu has been going around. That's all right, Mrs. Craig. I'll have Robert ride Thor, to give him some exercise. Yes, and I hope Hillary will be feeling better soon."

So Hillary wasn't at her jumping lesson because she was sick with the flu.

Cassie and Amy had made plans to go to the mall right after Cassie's lesson. Mrs. Lin and Amy stopped by the barn to pick her up.

"Any trouble with Hillary today?" Amy asked as Cassie slid into the back seat of the Lins' car.

"She didn't show up," Cassie said. "She has the flu."

"And its name is Thor," Amy added. "I bet she didn't want to ride him, and I don't blame her."

"Amy, I don't know where you get these ideas," Mrs. Lin said. "You barely know the girl, and you're already imagining what she's thinking."

Cassie shook her head. "I heard Trisha on the phone with Mrs. Craig. It sounded as if Hillary really is sick, Amy."

Amy rolled her eyes, but she didn't say anything else.

When they got to the mall, Mrs. Lin wanted to buy some towels at Lauren's Linens.

"Towels are so boring, Mom," Amy said. "Cassie

and I will look around, and meet you in . . .."

"In twenty minutes, in front of the fountain," Mrs. Lin said firmly. *"Twenty minutes*, Amy."

"Okay, Mom," Amy said, looking at her watch. "Where do you want to go, Cassie?"

"Boots and Saddles," Cassie replied immediately. The store sold everything a horsewoman might want: riding clothes, tack, trunks, grooming supplies. Cassie loved Boots and Saddles.

"Again?" Amy groaned, but she gave in. "Okay, eight minutes in Boots and Saddles, nine minutes in Dandelion looking at shorts and bathing suits, and three minutes buying some popcorn at the candy store. Let's hurry!"

The two of them raced up the middle aisle of the mall and burst through the door of Boots and Saddles.

"Hi, girls," said Linda, the salesperson. "We're having a sale on breeches and tights."

Cassie shook her head. "No, thanks. I want to buy a braiding kit."

She was planning ahead, to the first horse show, when she would be braiding Majesty's mane. The Lipizzan deserved his own supplies!

Because Cassie knew the store almost as well as she knew her own house, she found the braiding kit in less than three minutes. "Great. Let's look at the tights now," Amy said. "We have plenty of time."

The clothes were in the back part of the store, around a corner. Cassie and Amy were squeezing past a pile of hatboxes when Amy suddenly whispered, "Guess who's here. She doesn't look sick to me!"

It was Hillary, flipping through a rack of riding breeches. She looked healthy enough until she spotted Cassie and Amy. Then she started to look somewhat pale.

"Oh! Uh, hi," Hillary fumbled.

"Hi," said Cassie, and Amy just nodded.

"I didn't come to class today," Hillary began.

"I noticed," said Cassie.

"I wasn't feeling well. I had an awful headache." Hillary said.

"I heard it was the flu," Cassie said.

Hillary gulped. She looked as if she wanted to disappear. "Yes, well. That's what we thought at first."

"Are you feeling better now?" said Amy.

"Much," said Hillary. "I have to hurry. My mom is waiting."

"See you around," said Amy.

"Maybe I'll see you at the barn this week," said Cassie.

"Maybe," said Hillary. "By the way, you won't

mention this to Trisha, will you?" she added. "Running into me here at the mall, I mean. I really wouldn't want Trisha to think that I was, uh, goofing off or anything."

Cassie and Amy shook their heads, and Hillary rushed away.

Amy raised her eyebrows at Cassie.

"Okay, you were right," Cassie said to her friend. "Hillary didn't want to ride Thor."

"But if she doesn't ride him a lot, how can they ever get along any better?" Amy said.

"They can't," said Cassie. "I think Hillary chose the wrong horse for herself."

It made Cassie feel twice as lucky to have Majesty.

Cassie to the Rescue

Cassie didn't see Hillary at the barn for the next few days, even though she biked over to Birchwood every morning herself. After she warmed Majesty up, Cassie rode him over a course of jumps that Trisha had helped her set up in one of the outdoor rings. The course included single fences and combinations. Combinations were two or more fences with two or fewer strides between them.

The Lipizzan was used to clearing much higher fences. He was perfect every time on the two-and-a-half footers that Cassie had him jumping. In fact, Cassie felt that she was much more likely to mess *him* up on a course than the other way around.

Cassie knew many of her faults. Sometimes she forgot herself and looked down at the jump as Majesty took off. That made her body snap too far forward and could throw Majesty off balance. Or she might be trying so hard to hold herself straight that she stiffened up during the jump, which could make her collapse forward on the landing.

Trisha had advised, "When you're jumping, imagine landing with your *feet* on the ground, not your *seat*. Above all, though, don't make lists of everything you think you should be doing. Try to relax, just feel the horse, and enjoy yourself."

So Cassie had plenty to work on. That was why she didn't notice Hillary and Thor in the other outdoor ring on Thursday morning until after she heard a shriek.

Cassie had almost reached the end of her jumping course, and she didn't let herself lose her concentration. She stared straight ahead and didn't shift in the saddle until Majesty had sailed over the last jump in the course, and she'd brought him gently to a halt.

Then Cassie stood up in her stirrups and peered over the fence toward the second ring.

At the far end of that ring, someone had set up three low fences in a line. At first Cassie didn't notice

Hillary, only Thor. He was standing near the last fence, wild-eyed, his head thrust high in the air. Then the horse whirled around, and Cassie realized that Hillary was clinging to his neck.

Hillary had lost her left stirrup. She was almost completely out of the saddle, her left leg clamped halfway up Thor's side. And with Thor as nervy as he was, anything might happen!

"Hang on, Hillary!" Cassie called out. "I'm coming."

She slid out of her own saddle. Normally a rider would never leave a horse alone in the ring with its bridle on, but this was an emergency.

Cassie quickly twisted her reins into a figure eight and slipped the outer loop around Majesty's neck. Now he couldn't step on the reins and hurt himself.

Then she raced through the gate of her ring, scaled the fence of the second ring, and walked quietly toward Thor. Cassie didn't run, because she didn't want to upset the horse any further, or he might start running himself.

Hillary must have grabbed hold of the right rein at that point, because Thor suddenly began to spin in a circle to the right.

As Cassie reached them, she ordered, "Turn the rein loose, Hillary," a lot more calmly than she felt.

Thor was big and strong—and almost out of

control. Cassie couldn't move closer to the horse without getting trampled unless he stopped spinning. And he wouldn't stop spinning unless Hillary let go of the right rein.

"I . . . I can't!" Hillary yelled. "I'll fall off!"

"I can't help you until you let go," Cassie said.

Hillary must have made herself drop the rein. Thor stopped whirling around. He straightened out and took notice of Cassie.

She stretched her hand out and spoke to him softly, "Whoa. Easy. Easy, boy."

Thor's ears pricked forward, so Cassie knew he was focusing on her.

"Easy," Cassie said again, moving closer to him.

Hillary was still hanging onto Thor's neck on the right side. Her left knee was hooked over the saddle.

"Good boy," Cassie said to the horse.

The fingers of Cassie's left hand closed on the headstall of his bridle, and she held Thor steady. With her right hand, Cassie reached out and grabbed Hillary's ankle and pulled down.

With Cassie's help, Hillary managed to wriggle her way back into the saddle.

Hillary sat there for a second, staring straight ahead while she tried to catch her breath. Her face was totally drained of color, and she was trembling.

Suddenly she pulled her right foot out of the stirrup, swung her leg over, and slid off Thor.

"Are you okay?" Cassie asked Hillary once she was safely on the ground.

At first, Hillary just nodded, still tongue-tied with fright. Finally she murmured, "I'm fine. Thank you."

Cassie handed Hillary Thor's reins. It wasn't really any of her business, but Cassie asked anyway. "Why don't you try another horse? If a leased horse doesn't work out, you can usually trade it in for one that . . ."

"No! I can win on Thor. I know I can!" Hillary exclaimed.

Then she gazed at Cassie through narrowed eyes. Did she really believe that Cassie was just trying to think of ways to beat her?

"We have a few kinks to work out, but I'm keeping this horse," Hillary said. "You can be sure of that!"

"A few kinks? More like a major disaster waiting to happen!" Cassie was thinking. But she shrugged and said, "I hope it works out for you and Thor. See you later."

As she started across the ring toward the gate, Hillary called after her, "You'd better not tell Trisha about this, either!"

Cassie walked Majesty around for a few minutes, cooling him down and cooling herself down, too. She

91

had better things to do than tattle on Hillary. Then she led Majesty back to the barn and unsaddled him. She had just carried the saddle into the tack room when she heard an angry voice from inside the barn. A second later, Hillary stormed toward her.

"You had to do it, didn't you?" Hillary yelled. "You had to tell Trisha about Thor!"

As far as Cassie was concerned, Hillary was talking more nonsense! "I didn't say any . . . ," Cassie began.

But Hillary wouldn't listen. "Now I have to give him up. My stepfather is going to be so disappointed. I've let him down, and it's all thanks to you!" Hillary shouted. "You're a real creep, Cassie Sinclair!"

"Hillary, it's not what you think."

"I never had a chance around here," Hillary continued. "You're Trisha's favorite. Her precious Cassie can't do a thing wrong."

Cassie turned her back on Hillary. It was useless to argue with her. Besides, what Hillary said wasn't even true. Trisha didn't play favorites. She was fair to everyone.

Even though Cassie had turned her back, Hillary continued to rant. "She wouldn't let me ride Majesty, and now she won't let me ride Thor. And it's all your fault!"

Cassie spun around, her eyes flashing. "My fault?"

"Your fault!" Hillary repeated. "If I'd gotten Majesty to ride, the way I should have, none of this would have happened!"

"Do you know what?" Cassie said, sick of Hillary's attitude. "You're . . . you're just impossible!"

An Unexpected Visitor

"And then what?" Amy asked, when Cassie called to tell her about it later.

"I finished grooming Majesty, and Hillary stormed off in a huff," Cassie answered. "She's probably complaining to her parents right now. Hillary thinks everyone is out to get her, but the truth is she's her own worst enemy."

"Do you think she'll apologize to you?" Amy wanted to know.

"Hillary? You have to be kidding!" Cassie said. "Remember the good old days, Amy? Before Hillary Craig showed up, there was never this kind of tension at the stable. Now whenever I go there my stomach is completely tied up in knots."

"Maybe we should tell Trisha how we feel about Hillary," Amy said.

"What can Trisha do? Speak to Mr. and Mrs. Craig? They think Hillary is wonderful just the way she is. I tell you, Amy, I'd be really happy if I never had to see Hillary Craig again!" Cassie said. "And that's the truth!"

And for a few days, it seemed as though Cassie might get her wish.

On Friday morning, Cassie and Majesty had the outdoor rings to themselves. They were finishing a perfect ride around their jumping course when a white horse van rolled up to the barn. Cassie stopped Majesty beside the fence in time to see Robert leading Thor out of the barn. Trisha was following them.

She talked to the van driver. Then Robert loaded Thor into the white van and closed the tailgate. The van rolled back down the lane to the road.

"No more Thor," Cassie murmured to herself. But did that also mean *no more Hillary?*

Only Cassie, Amy, and Sara showed up for the Saturday group lesson.

"I'm dying to ask Trisha about Hillary," Amy whispered to Cassie while they waited for their turns. "But I don't have the nerve."

Cassie didn't have the nerve to ask, either. Not even when Hillary didn't come to her jumping class on Sunday.

By this time, Cassie wasn't sure exactly *how* she felt about it. She'd said to Amy that she'd be happy never to see Hillary again. But would she?

Cassie had to admit that having Hillary around had kept her on her toes. It had made Cassie try a little bit harder every time she rode.

And she felt just the teeniest bit bad for Hillary, too. Hillary was a good rider. It would be a shame if she gave it up completely.

Of course, Cassie wasn't spending all of her time thinking about Hillary Craig. Mostly she was thinking about getting ready for the first horse show, the one at Barker Farm, now only two weeks away.

Besides riding Majesty nearly every day, Cassie started doing exercises at home, such as lying on her back on the floor of the sunporch and doing scissor kicks in the air to strengthen the muscles in her back. Strong back muscles would help her to sit straighter in the saddle and to keep her balance better going over jumps.

Cassie was busy exercising when the doorbell rang at her house on Monday afternoon, the week after Hillary's mishap on Thor.

"Mom?" Cassie called out from the sunporch and kept touching her toes.

But Mrs. Sinclair was working at the computer in her home office.

The doorbell rang again.

"Coming!" Cassie yelled.

She hurried through the kitchen and living room and opened the front door. Hillary Craig stood on her front steps, looking down at her shoes.

"Hello," Hillary mumbled.

"Hello," Cassie said coolly. She couldn't imagine why Hillary was there.

Hillary cleared her throat. "Trisha said I had to apologize to you if I wanted to keep taking lessons at Birchwood," she mumbled at last. "So, I'm sorry for the way I've been acting."

Cassie nodded. That certainly explained Hillary's visit. And now that Hillary had done what Trisha had told her to do, Cassie fully expected her to leave.

But she didn't. Hillary went on, "I have some things to say myself, too." She stared down at the steps for a few seconds, then added: "You were right about Thor. Even though he *looked* great, he was too big and too high-strung for me. But it made me angry to have to admit it."

Cassie waited for her to continue.

98

"Trisha told me that you didn't say anything to her about Thor. It was Jane Clark," Hillary said.

"It's a good thing Jane did." Cassie said firmly. "You could have gotten hurt with that horse!"

"And you kept me from getting hurt that day," said Hillary, this time looking straight at Cassie. "I wanted to thank you again for that."

"Sure," said Cassie. She was starting to feel a little uncomfortable herself with all of these "thank you's," and "sorry's."

"How did you get here, anyway?" she asked Hillary, because there was no car waiting in the driveway. Cassie didn't see a bike leaning against the fence, either.

"My mom dropped me off on her way to the post office," Hillary said. "She'll be back for me in about ten minutes."

"Do you want to come in?" said Cassie.

"All right," Hillary said, and she followed Cassie into the house.

"Did I hear the bell?" Mrs. Sinclair was just walking into the living room. "Oh, hello."

"This is Hillary Craig, Mom," Cassie said, raising an eyebrow at her mother.

"Nice to meet you, Hillary," said Mrs. Sinclair. "Cassie, there are sodas in the refrigerator, and there is also a pitcher of freshly made iced tea."

"Tea would be nice," Hillary said politely.

Soon Hillary was sitting at the Sinclairs' kitchen table, drinking iced tea and munching on a cookie, as if she dropped by all the time. But she seemed to have run out of things to say.

So Cassie decided to take a turn at doing some of the talking.

"Will you be riding Bliss again?" she asked Hillary.

"I don't think so. I'm going to try out the bay horse, the one from last week," said Hillary. "He's not very pretty."

"Pretty isn't as important as steady," said Cassie, although she was lucky enough to have both in Majesty. "You know, I think we might be able to help each other with our riding."

"How?" Hillary asked, looking interested.

"When I'm practicing on Majesty, riding him over the jumps, I can't tell if I'm sitting quite right, or if I'm leaning too far forward, or if my legs are straight under me," Cassie said. "I could use a trainer. Somebody to tell me what I'm doing wrong, the way Trisha does during class."

"So if we ride at the same time during the week, we can take turns watching each other," Hillary said. She thought about it for a second and then said, "I think that's a good idea."

A car horn honked outside.

"That's my mom," Hillary said, standing up. "Thanks for the soda."

"Sure," said Cassie, standing up, too.

"I'm supposed to be getting the bay horse back tomorrow," Hillary told her. "Do you want to meet me at the barn on Wednesday morning to ride?"

"That's good for me," Cassie said. "I usually get there around nine o'clock."

Hillary nodded and said, "I'll see you at nine on Wednesday then."

Cassie walked Hillary to the front door and watched her hurry down the sidewalk to the waiting car. Cassie didn't think she and Hillary were necessarily going to be friends, at least not any time soon. But she did think the two of them could do each other some good now, instead of creating bad feelings.

When Amy heard about the arrangement Cassie had made with Hillary, she said, "But what if Hillary tries to mess you up? You know, like telling you that you're doing something wrong when you aren't. And ruining your concentration, or whatever."

"I don't think she will," Cassie said. "Because she doesn't want me to mess *her* up. Hillary is serious about her riding. And she now realizes that she can use extra help as much as I can."

"Hillary can use it a lot more, if you ask me!" Amy said, remembering the scene with Thor.

When Cassie rolled up to Birchwood on her bike on Wednesday morning at nine, Hillary was already waiting for her outside the tack room. The stocky bay horse was saddled, and Hillary was ready to go.

"This is Decker," she told Cassie. "He's a Quarter Horse and Thoroughbred mix."

"He seems really nice," Cassie said, scratching Decker's head under his forelock.

"He is nice. He didn't try to dump me off once yesterday," Hillary said, smiling a little. "I rode him all afternoon, and I think I can do pretty well on him."

Decker waited calmly while Cassie tacked up. Then the girls led their horses to one of the outdoor rings, where a line of low jumps was set up.

"You go first," Hillary said.

So Cassie pointed Majesty at the jumps, barely nudged him with her legs, and off they went. The Lipizzan sailed over the jumps as if they were ground poles. Once Cassie and Majesty had completed the course, they trotted back to Hillary and Decker. Cassie waited to hear what Hillary had to say.

"You looked great," Hillary told her.

"I know *Majesty* looked great," Cassie said. "He

always does. But what about me? Was I sitting just right? How were my feet?"

"I think you could bring your heels down more," Hillary said. "Especially when you're going over the jump. Heels down more, and toe out a little."

She seemed nervous about how Cassie might take it, but Cassie was pleased. "That's exactly the kind of thing I need to hear," she told Hillary.

Then it was Hillary's turn. Decker didn't have the stride that Majesty did. His legs were shorter, and so was his body. But he jumped neatly over the fences without flouncing or bouncing. And Hillary stayed centered in the saddle, her eyes straight ahead.

"How were we?" Hillary asked, after she'd trotted back to Cassie and Majesty.

Now Cassie felt a bit unsure about saying what she really thought about the ride. But she dove right in: "Well, I think you're a little heavy on the reins when you're going to a jump. And you're not really following his head with your hands once you've cleared the fence."

Cassie waited to see if Hillary would argue with her or get annoyed. Then they would be right back where they started.

But Hillary had listened to every word, and now she nodded. "Thanks," she said to Cassie. "That's just the kind of thing I need to know. Shall we do it again?"

"Let's," said Cassie.

She and Hillary didn't have to become best friends. After all, Cassie already *had* a best friend. But it was going to be great not having Hillary for an enemy.

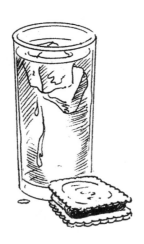

The Horse Show

On the day of the horse show at Barker Farm, Trisha wanted all of the girls in the Saturday group to be at Birchwood Stable at six-thirty in the morning. The first classes at the show would be starting at nine o'clock. And it would take the girls quite some time to groom their horses, braid their horses' manes, and get them loaded into a van to travel to Barker Farm.

Cassie got to Birchwood at six that morning. She was so keyed up about riding Majesty in the show that she'd been ready to go since five-fifteen.

But Hillary was ahead of her. She was already leading Decker out to the grooming tree when Mr. Sinclair and Cassie pulled into the parking area that was located beside the barn.

"Hi!" Hillary called out as Cassie jumped out of the car.

"Hi!" Cassie called back. She grabbed her riding clothes out of the back seat: a black jacket, beige breeches, black boots, a white shirt with a white stock tie and gold pin, and black gloves. Her hat completed her outfit.

"Good luck, kid," Mr. Sinclair said to his daughter. "We'll see you at the show. We're rooting for you." He waved good-bye and drove away, yawning.

Cassie carried her clothes to Trisha's office, said hello to Trisha, and hurried to Majesty's stall. The Lipizzan had finished his breakfast and seemed to be waiting for her. Maybe he had sensed the excitement, because some of Trisha's other students were rushing here and there inside the barn, getting ready.

Cassie haltered Majesty and led him out to the grooming tree. She and Hillary had finished brushing their horses and were picking out their hooves when Amy and Sara arrived together by car with Sara's mom. Sara was so nervous about riding in public that her eyes looked ready to pop right out of her chalk-white face.

Not Amy. Amy was still only half-awake. She smiled sleepily at Cassie and said, "I don't know how you can move so fast at this time of day."

But with Cassie's help, Amy had Freckles groomed and braided and ready to be loaded into the van by seven-thirty. Then the girls changed into their riding clothes and piled into Trisha's station wagon along with two other kids. Thirty minutes later, they were pulling into the winding driveway of Barker Farm.

"Wow! So many people!" Amy said, staring out her window.

There were horse vans, horse trailers, cars, and trucks filling almost every inch of the large mowed field.

"Lots more than last year," Cassie agreed.

"And a big refreshment tent," Amy said. "I wonder if they'll have those incredible brownies again?"

Sara sighed and looked ready to faint. Food was the last thing on *her* mind!

"There's our van," Hillary said, pointing it out. "Decker's already unloaded."

Trisha drove the station wagon between two large trailers and pulled up beside the Birchwood horses.

"Here we are, girls," she said, opening her car door. "I'll pick up your numbers at the office. And remember, try to relax. Have some fun with this!"

Barker Farm had three outdoor rings, and at nine o'clock sharp, show classes started in two of them.

Little kids were riding in a line in the ring closest to the refreshment tent. In the middle ring, teenagers put their horses through the complicated movements of dressage.

Cassie would have liked to watch *everyone* doing *everything*. But she didn't have time.

Trisha came back with their numbers and pinned them to the backs of the girls' jackets. Cassie was "contestant number 38." Then Trisha walked the jumping course with Cassie and Hillary. It was set up in the third ring.

There were eight jumps arranged in a loose figure-eight pattern. Trisha helped Cassie and Hillary count how many strides their horses should be making before taking off over each of the jumps. Sometimes it was two strides; sometimes it was three or more.

After that, Cassie rode Majesty around in an open area to warm him up and loosen up his muscles so he'd be ready. The Lipizzan paid no attention to noisy kids, or dogs, or nickering horses, or the slamming of car doors and tailgates. He was all business, his ears turning back toward Cassie for any instructions she might have.

Amy and Freckles were walking around in a circle, taking in the sights. And now that Sara was mounted on Charlie, she'd gotten some of her color back. She even managed a smile at Cassie.

Cassie glanced over at Hillary and Decker. The bay horse was trotting along as calmly as if he were in the indoor ring at Birchwood. Cassie couldn't imagine *what* Thor would have been doing by now, but she was fairly certain that it wouldn't have been what Hillary wanted.

Then a voice on the loudspeaker announced the class that Amy and Sara would be riding in.

"Good luck!" Cassie and Hillary called out to both of them.

It seemed as though only seconds had passed before Amy was back, standing at the edge of the open space and waving a yellow ribbon at Cassie: "I won third!" she yelled. "And check out Sara!"

Sara was right behind her, proudly holding up a blue ribbon. "Way to go!" Cassie yelled back.

"Congratulations!" Hillary called to them.

In a few more minutes, the Beginning Equitation-Over-Fences class was announced. That was the class that Cassie and Hillary would be competing in.

The two girls looked at each other. "That's us," Cassie said, her heart pounding.

"Best of luck," Hillary said. And she sounded as if she meant it.

Cassie didn't watch the first two contestants jumping the course. She didn't try to spot her parents in the crowd, either. Instead, she tried to focus on relaxing by doing some deep breathing and walking Majesty slowly around.

Then the ring steward called out, "Number 15," Hillary's number.

Cassie moved Majesty closer to the ring. She couldn't see much of the course from where she was standing, but she did see Decker clearing the fifth and sixth fences like a pro. And Hillary followed his head with her hands on the way down, just as Cassie had told her to in practice.

When Hillary completed the course, the crowd around the ring broke into applause. As she rode Decker back through the gate, Mr. and Mrs. Craig hurried up to her. Mr. Craig gave Hillary a hug, and she looked ready to burst with pleased excitement.

Another girl rode through the course. Then the ring steward called Cassie's number.

"Show time," Cassie murmured to Majesty.

First she trotted him quietly into the ring and made a small, smooth circle. Then Cassie nudged Majesty into a canter and headed toward the first jump. It was a single pole, and Majesty cleared it effortlessly.

The Lipizzan turned to the left, and to the left again, and approached a combination fence, which was really two fences with two strides in between them. Cassie looked straight ahead and kept in touch with Majesty's mouth through the reins. They made perfect jumps over the combination.

The next fence was five strides away. Majesty felt to Cassie as though he might be moving a little too quickly, so she gave the slightest tug on the reins. Then he soared over the third fence, turned left, and turned left again to line up with the fourth fence, which was an oxer.

Oxers are wide jumps made with two separate fences and a little space in between them. For Cassie, an oxer was the scariest kind of jump, because she always felt that her horse might not make it across the open space to clear the second fence.

But she trusted Majesty to know what he was doing. All Cassie really had to worry about, she told herself, was sitting properly so that she wouldn't throw the Lipizzan off balance. And not looking down!

Cassie remembered her practices with Hillary and worked on keeping her heels down, her toes out, and her back straight, as she and Majesty took off over the wide jump. She tried to become a part of her horse.

And Majesty did a beautiful job, his head down, his knees up, his lower legs tight. His ears were pricked forward, his eyes already focusing on the next jump. And he cleared the oxer easily.

After the oxer, the rest of the course was a breeze. When Cassie cantered across the finish line, there was a roar from the crowd. She could pick out Amy's voice yelling, "Yay, Cassie!"

As soon as Cassie rode out of the gate, her parents rushed over to her.

"I've never been so proud in my life as when you sailed over that wide jump!" her dad said.

And her mom added, "I didn't know whether to close my eyes or keep them open, so I just crossed my fingers and held my breath."

"You were excellent!" Amy said when she joined them. "Good work, Majesty," she added, patting the horse's neck. And Majesty bobbed his head up and down as if he were agreeing with her.

The last girl rode, and the class was over. It took the judge a few minutes to check her scores and hand the results to the ring steward.

Cassie glanced around for Hillary and spotted her with Decker, standing at the far side of the ring with the Craigs. Hillary saw Cassie and held one hand up in the air with her fingers crossed.

"Sixth place goes to number 23!" the ring steward called out.

A girl on a tall gray gelding rode into the ring to pick up her green ribbon.

The ring steward called out the number for the fifth-place winner, then fourth, then third. Cassie was beginning to worry, especially when he got to second place and announced, "The second place ribbon goes to . . . number 15!"

"That's Hillary," Cassie said to her parents and Amy. And her heart sank, because she couldn't imagine doing better than second place!

Hillary had a wide smile on her face as the steward fastened a red ribbon to Decker's headstall. Her parents were beaming, too.

The ring steward paused for a minute to allow Hillary to ride out of the ring. Then he called out, "The blue ribbon for first place for this event goes to . . ." He looked down at the paper he was holding, and continued, "contestant number . . . 38!"

Cassie almost couldn't believe her ears!

"That's you, Cassie!" Amy squealed.

"Congratulations, sweetie!" said Mrs. Sinclair.

"Get in there, honey," said Mr. Sinclair, giving her a pat on the knee.

As she rode Majesty toward the gate, Cassie saw

Hillary waiting beside it for her.

"You made a great ride. You deserve first!" Hillary said.

"Thanks," Cassie said, smiling at her.

But Cassie knew exactly who deserved the blue: Majesty, her Lipizzan!

FACTS
ABOUT THE BREED

You probably know a lot about Lipizzan horses from reading this book. Here are some more interesting facts about this special breed.

∩ Lipizzans generally stand between 14.2 and 16.1 hands high. Instead of using feet and inches, all horses are measured in hands. A hand is equal to four inches.

∩ Lipizzans get their name from a town in the former Yugoslavia. In Lipizza (or Lipica), Austria's Archduke Charles II bred the first Lipizzans from horses that he had imported from Spain.

∩ The most famous Lipizzans are the performing stallions of Vienna's Spanish Riding School. The school is called

"Spanish" in honor of the horses that the Archduke first brought from that country in 1580.

∩ Since 1735, the Spanish School has had its own imposing building in downtown Vienna. The school is housed in part of the Hofburg Palace. Even the stables at the school look like part of a palace. The horses eat from red marble mangers.

∩ Traditionally, the training of a Lipizzan begins late. The horses of the Spanish School are allowed to frolic in the pastures until they are four years old.

∩ A young Lipizzan first learns to work on a lunge line, a long rein that allows the horse to move around the trainer in a large circle. Then the horse learns to perform the *piaffe,* a delicate prancing trot that is done in place, and also a *pirouette,* like a ballerina.

∩ Talented horses go on to learn the "airs above the ground." In the *levade*, the horse bends his hind legs and raises his chest and forelegs off the ground so that he looks like a marble statue about to leap into action.

∩ Next comes the *courbette*. Starting in the *levade* position, the horse jumps forward on his hind legs and lands on his hind legs. All the while, his forelegs are kept neatly tucked under the chest. The strongest horses can perform ten of these difficult jumps in a row.

∩ In the *croupade*, the horse leaps into the air and tucks all four feet underneath him.

∩ The *ballotade*, like the *croupade*, is executed by jumping into the air. In this move, however, the horse turns his hind feet up so the viewer can see the bottoms of his gleaming hooves.

∩ The *capriole* is probably the most spectacular of the "high-school movements." Like the winged Pegasus of the Greek myth, the horse leaps into the air. At the very height of his jump, he kicks out his hind legs and truly looks as if he can fly. The horse does land, though, and on all four feet.

∩ While Lipizzans are slow to mature, they live a long time. Some of the stallions performing with the Spanish School are more than 20 years old.

∩ Lipizzans are great performers and are also becoming popular private horses. Many Lipizzan owners practice dressage or drive small carriages. Others find that the Lipizzan's sensible temperament and great loyalty make these alabaster beauties superior riding horses.